The Fury of Darth Maul
GAME BOOK

The galaxy is yours.
Be a part of

STAR WARS®

EPISODE I
ADVENTURES

#1 Search for the Lost Jedi
#2 The Bartokk Assassins
#3 The Fury of Darth Maul

. . . and more to come!

STAR WARS®

EPISODE I

ADVENTURES

GAME BOOK

The Fury of Darth Maul

Ryder Windham

SCHOLASTIC INC.

ISBN 0-439-12986-9

12 11 10 9 8 7 6 5 4 3 2 1   9/9 0 1 2 3 4/0

Printed in the U.S.A.
First Scholastic printing, November 1999

The Fury of Darth Maul
GAME BOOK

YOUR ADVENTURE BEGINS!

For the full story behind your adventure, read up to page 40 in your Star Wars Adventures novel *The Fury of Darth Maul*. Or begin here.

You are Darth Maul or the assassin droid C-3PX. The Adventure Guide contains the rules of *Star Wars Adventures.* You must follow these rules at all times.

According to Neimoidian spies on Esseles, the fifty Trade Federation droid starfighters and prototype hyperdrive engine were stolen by a Bartokk freighter. You have tracked the freighter to a fortress on the planet Ralltiir, and allowed yourself to be taken prisoner in order to infiltrate the Bartokk hive.

The Bartokks are preparing to deploy twenty-five droid starfighters to attack the planet Corulag. If they succeed, the Trade Federation will be blamed for the attack.

You cannot let this happen.

You have also learned the Bartokks possess scanner technology that allows them to track the Sith Infiltrator when it is in cloak-mode. The Bartokks intend to seize the Infiltrator, which remains in the canyon below the fortress. The secrets of the Sith must be protected. You cannot allow the Infiltrator to fall into enemy hands.

You are locked in a cell with your hands in restraints. You must escape and carry out the commands of Darth Sidious. Your goals are to learn who hired the Bartokks, retrieve the Trade Federation property, and destroy the Bartokks. You also must prevent the droid starfighters from reaching their destination, and stop the Bartokks from taking the Infiltrator.

Furthermore, you will try to steal the Bartokks' tracking sensor technology so you can incorporate it into the Infiltrator's defense systems. With this technology, you can modify your starship's cloaking device to resist Bartokk scans. Although stealing the Bartokks' sensor technology is not crucial to your assignment, you will be rewarded with a bonus if you succeed.

There are fifteen Bartokks in every assassin team. The black-armored insectoids are fierce killers, and extremely difficult to defeat. Your orders are to eliminate all of them.

4

*　　*　　*

Choose your character. Every character has unique talents that are listed on each character card. As a Sith Lord, Darth Maul is strongly allied with the dark side of the Force.

C-3PX has the advantage of being an expert marksman who is equipped with numerous concealed weapons. Although he does not carry his own lightsaber, he knows how to use one. Like other protocol droids, C-3PX is a skilled communicator and speaks over six million languages.

As C-3PX, you can take as many weapons and devices as you want. As any other character, you can take no more than three weapons and devices (one must be a lightsaber). NOTE: The Bartokk has put a restraining bolt on C-3PX; although the droid can defy the restraint program, the bolt has disabled his ability to use his concealed weapons. C-3PX cannot use any of his weapons until he gets the restraining bolt activator from the Bartokk. The same Bartokk also took away Darth Maul's lightsaber, so you cannot use a lightsaber until you retrieve it from the Bartokk.

5

You can take two vehicles (one for space, one for land). You can use Power three times on this adventure.

You start this adventure with your Adventure Point (AP) total from your previous adventure, or 1000 AP if this is your first adventure.

May the power of the Sith Lords guide you.

YOUR ADVENTURE:

THE FURY OF
DARTH MAUL

Within the confines of the wretched cell, the interrogator droid hovers a few centimeters away from you, then trains its socketed photoreceptor on your face. The droid stares at you, then snickers. "Think you're tough, huh? When I'm done with you, you'll be singing a different tune."

Behind your back, your wrists are secured by durasteel binders. You take a step backward, and your left hand brushes against a thin metal wire sticking out of the wall.

You must break free of your restraints. Choose to quickly hot-wire the binder's lock or break the binders (with or without Power).

To hot-wire the binder's lock: Roll the 10-dice to use the wire to short the lock. Your roll# + your skill# is your adventure#.

If your adventure# is equal to or more than 6, add the difference to your AP total. The binders snap open and fall to the floor. You may proceed.

If your adventure# is less than 6, subtract the difference from your AP total. The binders lock is pick-proof. Proceed to break the durasteel binders (below).

To break the durasteel binders (using Power)*: Choose your Alteration Power. Roll the 10-dice to open the binders. Your roll# + your strength# + your Power# + your Power's low-resist# is your adventure#.

If your adventure# is equal to or more than 8, add the difference to your AP total. The binders shatter and fall to the filthy floor. You may proceed.

If your adventure# is less than 8, subtract the difference from your AP total. You'll have to break the binders without Power (below).

*NOTE: This counts as one of three Power uses you are allowed on this adventure.

To break the binders (without Power): Roll the 10-dice to use your own strength to free your hands from the binders. Your roll# + your strength# is your adventure#.

If your adventure# is equal to or more than 7, add the difference to your AP total. You flex your arms, forcing your wrists apart. The binders split and fall to the filthy floor. You may proceed.

If your adventure# is less than 7, subtract the difference from your AP total. The binders are composed of a dense durasteel composite. It will require enormous strength to break them. To use more strength, roll the 10-dice for your new roll#. Your new roll# + your strength# + 1 is your new adventure#.

If your new adventure# is equal to or more than 7, add the difference to your AP total. You force your arms apart and the binders break away from your wrists. You may proceed.

If your new adventure# is less than 7, subtract the difference from your AP total. Go back to "roll the 10-dice for your new roll#" and repeat. When you have broken the binders, you may proceed.

The interrogator droid makes an excited whirring sound. It is startled to see you have freed yourself. The droid activates its laser scalpels and hurtles through the air toward you. Choose to dodge or kick the interrogator droid.

To dodge the interrogator droid: Roll the 10-dice to leap away from the oncoming droid. If evasion is one of your talents, your roll# + your stealth# + 2 is your adventure#. If evasion is not one of your talents, your roll# + your stealth# is your adventure#.

If your adventure# is equal to or more than 7, add the difference to your AP total. As you leap aside, the droid races past you and smashes hard against the cell wall. You may proceed.

If your adventure# is less than 7, subtract the difference from your AP total. The droid anticipates your action, and pulls back before it strikes the cell wall. Then it prepares for another attack. Proceed to kick the interrogator droid (below).

To kick the interrogator droid: Roll the 20-dice to launch a well-placed kick at the hovering droid. If maneuvering is one of your talents, your roll# + your strength# + 2 is your adventure#. If maneuvering is not one of your talents, your roll# + your strength# is your adventure#.

If your adventure# is equal to or more than 13, add the difference to your AP total. Your kick connects with the droid, sending the shrieking machine on a collision course with the cell's ceiling. The droid bashes against the ceiling, then plummets and crashes to the floor. You may proceed.

If your adventure# is less than 13, subtract the difference from your AP total. Your kick missed the droid. Go back to "Roll the 20-dice to launch a well-placed kick" and repeat. When you have defeated the droid, you may proceed.

Although your fight with the droid causes plenty of noise, the Bartokk guards do not burst into the cell. Either the cell walls are soundproof or the Bartokks are confident you just lost.

Smoke rises from the deactivated interrogator droid. You step over its smoldering parts and examine the cell door. Locked from the outside, the door is heavily reinforced.

As you consider your options, you study the remains of the interrogation droid. Its electroshock assembly and sonic torture device are undamaged. From these components, you could construct a small explosive device. One of the droid's laser scalpels is also intact, and you might be able to use it to cut through the door.

The droid's interrogation serum is also intact, so you unclamp it from the droid's body. You'll save it for later. With any luck, it might work on a Bartokk.

To open the cell door, choose to use Power, use a laser scalpel, or construct an explosive device. If you choose to construct an explosive device, you will also be required to activate it.

To open the cell door (using Power)*: Choose your Alteration Power or Infiltration Power. Roll the 20-dice to open the locking bolt. Your roll# + your skill# + your Power# + your Power's low-resist# is your adventure#.

If your adventure# is equal to or more than 14, add the difference to your AP total. The cell door opens. You may proceed.

If your adventure# is less than 14, subtract the difference from your AP total. The cell door is jammed shut. Proceed to use a laser scalpel (below) or construct an explosive device (next page).

*NOTE: This counts as one of three Power uses you are allowed on this adventure.

To use a laser scalpel: Roll the 10-dice to cut through the cell door. Your roll# + your skill# is your adventure#.

If your adventure# is equal to or more than 7, add the difference to your AP total. Your expert use of the laser scalpel enables you to cut a large hole through the door. You may proceed.

If your adventure# is less than 7, subtract the difference from your AP total. The cell door is more dense than you realized, so creating a hole will require a stronger laser beam. To increase the power of the laser scalpel, roll the 10-dice for your new roll#. Your new roll# + your skill + 1 is your new adventure#.

If your new adventure# is equal to or more than 7, add 1 AP to your AP total. Within seconds, you carve a hole in the door. You may proceed.

If your new adventure# is less than 7, subtract the difference from your AP total. The laser scalpel shorts out. You decide to conserve your own arsenal and improvise with the deactivated interrogator droid's other parts. Proceed to construct an explosive device (below).

To construct an explosive device: Roll the 20-dice to remove and rewire the deactivated droid's electroshock assembly and sonic torture device. Your roll# + your knowledge# + your skill# is your adventure#.

If your adventure# is equal to or more than 11, add the difference to your AP total. You have successfully transformed the droid's parts into a small but powerful bomb. Scooping some sticky slime from the cell floor, you use it to secure the bomb to the door. Proceed to activate the explosive device (below).

If your adventure# is less than 11, subtract the difference from your AP total. You fumble with the droid's parts. Go back to "Roll the 20-dice to remove and rewire" and repeat.

To activate the explosive device: Roll the 10-dice to trigger the small bomb. Your roll# + your skill# is your adventure#.

If your adventure# is equal to or more than 5, add the difference to your AP total. As you slip under the metal bed for protection, the bomb detonates and tears a wide hole through the cell door. You may proceed.

If your adventure# is less than 5, subtract 10 AP from your AP total. The slime you used to stick the bomb to the door wasn't sticky enough. The bomb falls from the door and rolls toward you. The bomb will explode within seconds! To pick it up and throw it at the door, roll the 10-dice again for your new roll#. Your new roll# + your skill# + your strength# is your new adventure#.

If your new adventure# is equal to or more than 9, add the difference to your AP total.

You grab the bomb from under the metal bed and throw it at the door just in time. The bed frame shields your body as the bomb blows a hole clear through the cell door. You may proceed.

If your new adventure# is less than 9, subtract the difference from your AP total. Without any time left to throw the bomb, you are forced to quickly deactivate it. Now you must try again. Go back to "Roll the 10-dice to trigger the small bomb" and repeat. When you have blown open the door, you may proceed.

You step out of the cell and onto the corridor's grated floor. Although four Bartokks brought you and your ally into the dungeon, only two Bartokk escorts are posted outside the cells. The other cell doors remain sealed. The two Bartokks whirl to confront you. Choose to evade the two Bartokks, combat both Bartokks at once, or combat one Bartokk at a time.

To evade the two Bartokks: Roll the 10-dice to throw open another cell door and enter the cell. If evasion is one of your talents, your roll# + your stealth# + 1 is your adventure#. If evasion is not one of your talents, your roll# + your stealth# is your adventure#.

If your adventure# is equal to or more than 8, add the difference to your AP total. You hide under the metal bed as the two Bartokks enter the cell. When you hear that cell's interrogation droid lowering, you scramble out of the cell and slam the door shut. The Bartokks are trapped with the interrogation droid, and you may proceed.

If your adventure# is less than 8, subtract the difference from your AP total. The cell door is locked and you can't get in. Proceed to combat both Bartokks at once (below).

To combat both Bartokks at once: Roll the 20-dice to jump between the two Bartokks. Your roll# + your stealth# + your strength# is your adventure#.

If your adventure# is equal to or more than 14, add the difference to your AP total. Standing between the Bartokks, you duck as they fire their poison-tipped arrows. They accidentally shoot each other, and the two insectoid assassins collapse to the floor. You may proceed.

If your adventure# is less than 14, subtract the difference from your AP total. Holding their fire, both Bartokks take a cautious step sideways so you are no longer standing between them. Proceed to combat one Bartokk at a time (below).

To combat one Bartokk at a time: Roll the 20-dice to jump beside one Bartokk and snatch a poison-tipped arrow from the assassin's quiver. If maneuvering is one of your talents, your roll# + your stealth# + your strength# + 1 is your adventure#. If maneuvering is not one of your talents, your roll# + your stealth# + your strength# is your adventure#.

If your adventure# is equal to or more than 15, add the difference to your AP total. You snatch the arrow and plunge the poison tip into the Bartokk's torso, and the creature falls to the grated floor. Go back to "Roll the 20-dice to jump beside one Bartokk" and repeat for the second Bartokk. When you have defeated both Bartokks, you may proceed.

If your adventure# is less than 15, subtract 9 AP from your AP total. It will require more strength to drive the arrow tip through the Bartokk's armor-plated body. To use more strength, roll the 20-dice again for your new roll#. If maneuvering is one of your talents, your new roll# + your stealth# + your strength# + 2 is your new adventure#. If maneuvering is not one of your talents, your new roll# + your stealth# + your strength# + 1 is your new adventure#.

If your new adventure# **is**
than 15, add 2 AP to **yo**
pierce the Bartokk's arm**o**
remains, go back to "Ro**ll**
for your new roll#" and **re**
Bartokks are defeated, **yo**

If your new adventure# **is**
tract the difference from **y**
must break through **the**
plating. Go back to "Ro**ll**
for your new roll#" **a**
you have defeated bot**h a**
proceed.

Since the other cell do**or**
it appears your ally is st**ill**
about to attempt to free **yo**
other two Bartokk esco**rt**
end of the corridor. See**i**
over their fallen comrad**es,**
tokks reaches to the **wa**
panel that controls a **ser**
within the dungeon. Sudd**c**
floor drops away beneat**h**
out any chance to lea**p**
plunge down through th**e t**
a dark cavern.

You land on top of a **sa**

them. Proceed to combat one Bartokk at a time (below).

To combat one Bartokk at a time: Roll the 20-dice to jump beside one Bartokk and snatch a poison-tipped arrow from the assassin's quiver. If maneuvering is one of your talents, your roll# + your stealth# + your strength# + 1 is your adventure#. If maneuvering is not one of your talents, your roll# + your stealth# + your strength# is your adventure#.

If your adventure# is equal to or more than 15, add the difference to your AP total. You snatch the arrow and plunge the poison tip into the Bartokk's torso, and the creature falls to the grated floor. Go back to "Roll the 20-dice to jump beside one Bartokk" and repeat for the second Bartokk. When you have defeated both Bartokks, you may proceed.

If your adventure# is less than 15, subtract 9 AP from your AP total. It will require more strength to drive the arrow tip through the Bartokk's armor-plated body. To use more strength, roll the 20-dice again for your new roll#. If maneuvering is one of your talents, your new roll# + your stealth# + your strength# + 2 is your new adventure#. If maneuvering is not one of your talents, your new roll# + your stealth# + your strength# + 1 is your new adventure#.

If your new adventure# is equal to or more than 15, add 2 AP to your AP total. You pierce the Bartokk's armor. If one Bartokk remains, go back to "Roll the 20-dice again for your new roll#" and repeat. When both Bartokks are defeated, you may proceed.

If your new adventure# is less than 15, subtract the difference from your AP total. You must break through the Bartokk's armor plating. Go back to "Roll the 20-dice again for your new roll#" and repeat. After you have defeated both assassins, you may proceed.

Since the other cell doors remain sealed, it appears your ally is still trapped. You are about to attempt to free your ally when the other two Bartokk escorts appear at the end of the corridor. Seeing you standing over their fallen comrades, one of the Bartokks reaches to the wall and strikes a panel that controls a series of trapdoors within the dungeon. Suddenly, the grated floor drops away beneath your feet. Without any chance to leap to safety, you plunge down through the trapdoor and into a dark cavern.

You land on top of a sandpile and roll to

the subterranean floor. Lifting yourself up, you look at the cavern ceiling. The trapdoor seals, but you can see two Bartokks through the grated floor. The Bartokks scurry across the corridor and jam twin-bolt crossbows down through the floor's open slots. They aim their weapons at you and fire. Four poison-tipped, armor-piercing arrows speed toward you.

Choose to dodge or catch the arrows. After you retrieve the arrows, you will be able to hurl them back at the Bartokks.

To dodge the arrows: Roll the 10-dice to jump to the side and avoid being struck. If evasion is one of your talents, your roll# + your stealth# + 2 is your adventure#. If evasion is not one of your talents, your roll# + your stealth# + 1 is your adventure#.

If your adventure# is equal to or more than 8, add the difference to your AP total. Four arrows stick into the ground near your feet. You yank two arrows out of the ground. Proceed to hurl the arrows back at the two Bartokks (next page).

If your adventure# is less than 8, subtract the difference from your AP total. It suddenly occurs to you that some Bartokks use explosive arrows. If such arrows strike the ground, you could be blown to bits. Proceed to catch the arrows (below).

To catch the arrows: Roll the 20-dice to snatch the four arrows by their shafts. Your roll# + your stealth# + your strength# is your adventure#.

If your adventure# is equal to or more than 14, add the difference to your AP total. Your hands move with lightning speed as you pluck each speeding arrow from the air. Proceed to hurl the arrows back at the two Bartokks (below).

If your adventure# is less than 14, subtract the difference from your AP total. Go back to "Roll the 20-dice to snatch the four arrows" and repeat. After you have caught them, proceed to hurl the arrows back at the two Bartokks (below).

To hurl the arrows back at the two Bartokks: Roll the 20-dice to throw two arrows up to the cavern ceiling and through the grated floor. If targeting is one of your talents, your roll# + your strength# + 2 is your adventure#. If targeting is not one of your talents, your roll# + your strength# + 1 is your adventure#.

If your adventure# is equal to or more than 14, add the difference to your AP total. The poison-tipped arrows pass through the narrow slits of the grated floor and strike the Bartokks. Both collapse with a loud clatter to the floor, and you may proceed.

If your adventure# is less than 14, subtract 8 AP from your AP total. You missed the Bartokks, but you have two arrows left. To throw your last two arrows at the Bartokks, roll the 20-dice again for your new roll#. If targeting is one of your talents, your new roll# + your strength# + 3 is your new adventure#. If targeting is not one of your talents, your new roll# + your strength# + 2 is your new adventure#.

If your new adventure# is equal to or more than 13, add the difference to your AP total. You fling the arrows up into the air, and they pass through the grated floor and strike the Bartokks. The Bartokks crash to the floor and you may proceed.

If your new adventure# is less than 13, subtract the difference from your AP total. The arrows hit the grating and fall back to the floor. Go back to "roll the 20-dice again for your new roll#" and repeat. When the poison-tipped arrows reach the Bartokks, you may proceed.

The trapdoor is sealed, and it is far too high for you to reach. You will have to find another way out of the cave.

For defeating four Bartokk assassins, add 90 AP to your AP total.

A loud hiss stirs the air. Turning, you see a shadow shift against the rough rock walls. A scaled head pushes forward from the darkness, and a pair of large green eyes stares down at you from behind a wide reptilian mouth.

It's a draigon-slug. The gigantic snake-like creatures have been discovered living in caves on several worlds, but you are surprised to find one beneath the surface of Ralltiir. Perhaps the Bartokks imported the beast and kept it to discourage thieves from entering the caves. Draigon-slugs are fire-breathing monsters, and they have been known to devour their prey in a single bite.

To your left, a tall stalagmite rises up from the cavern floor. The stalagmite might offer protective cover from the draigon-slug.

Choose to hide behind the stalagmite, tie the draigon-slug into a knot, or throw a rock at it.

To hide behind the stalagmite: Roll the 10-dice to dive behind the tall stalagmite. If evasion is one of your talents, your roll# + your stealth# + 2 is your adventure#. If evasion is not one of your talents, your roll# + your stealth# + 1 is your adventure#.

If your adventure# is equal to or more than 8, add the difference + 10 to your AP total. The draigon-slug is unable to find you behind the stalagmite. The creature loses interest and slithers away. You may proceed.

If your adventure# is less than 8, subtract 4 AP from your AP total. The draigon-slug slithers forward to follow you around the stalagmite. Unless you hide on the opposite side, the creature will find you. To hide on the other side of the stalagmite, roll the 10-dice again for your new roll#. If evasion is one of your talents, your new roll# + your stealth# + 3 is your new adventure#. If evasion is not one of your talents, your new roll# + your stealth# + 2 is your new adventure#.

If your new adventure# is equal to or more than 8, add the difference to your AP total.

Unable to find you, the draigon-slug recedes against the wall and does not attack. You may proceed.

If your new adventure# is less than 8, subtract the difference from your AP total. The creature anticipates your movement and weaves its head to the other side of the stalagmite. Fixing its eyes on you, the monster prepares to lunge. Proceed to tie the draigon-slug into a knot (below).

To tie the draigon-slug into a knot: Roll the 10-dice to run toward the draigon-slug, jump over its back, and grab the end of its tail. Your roll# + your strength# + 2 is your adventure#.

If your adventure# is equal to or more than 9, add the difference + 7 to your AP total. As the draigon-slug twists around to pursue you, you drag its tail toward its stomach, forcing the creature into a loop. Before the draigon-slug realizes what you're doing, you pull its tail around its looped body. The draigon-slug is tangled by its own form, and you may proceed.

If your adventure# is less than 9, subtract the difference from your AP total. The draigon-slug's tail is far too heavy for you to lift. Proceed to throw a rock at the draigon-slug (below).

To throw a rock at the draigon-slug: Roll the 20-dice to throw a large rock right between the creature's eyes. If targeting is one of your talents, your roll# + your strength# + 1 is your adventure#. If targeting is not one of your talents, your roll# + your strength# is your adventure#.

If your adventure# is equal to or more than 12, add the difference to your AP total. The hurled stone smacks against the draigon-slug's head, and the creature recoils in pain. It slithers off to hide behind a large boulder, and you may proceed.

If your adventure# is less than 12, subtract the difference from your AP total. You didn't throw the stone hard enough, and you have only angered the draigon-slug. It opens its mouth and exhales a concentrated burst of flames. To avoid being incinerated by the draigon-slug's fiery breath, roll the 20-dice again for your new roll#. If evasion is one of your talents, your new roll# + your stealth# + your strength# +1 is your new adventure#. If evasion is not one of your talents, your new roll# + your stealth# + your strength# is your new adventure#.

If your new adventure# is equal to or more than 14, add the difference to your AP total. You jump away just in time to avoid being burned by the draigon-slug's fire. Go back to "Roll the 20-dice to throw a large rock" and repeat. When you have defeated the draigon-slug, you may proceed.

If your new adventure# is less than 14, subtract the difference from your AP total. Turning its head after you, the draigon-slug continues to blast fire in your direction. Go back to "roll the 20-dice again for your new roll#" and repeat. When you have evaded the draigon-slug and struck it with a rock, you may proceed.

Leaving the draigon-slug behind, you try to find another way out of the cave. You step around a stalagmite and discover a tunnel entrance in the cavern wall.

You enter the tunnel. It leads into an underground chamber with a high vaulted ceiling. You see what appears to be another tunnel, but as you approach it, the path suddenly ends at a ledge. The ledge rides the edge of a broad, deep chasm. From the ledge to the next tunnel, the distance is only nine meters. It would be a dangerous jump, but not impossible.

Dozens of long, securely moored stalactites dangle from the chamber's ceiling. By gripping one tapered end of a stalactite after another, you should be able to travel hand-over-hand to the other side of the chasm. You are considering whether to jump the chasm or scale the ceiling when you see a mammoth spydr clinging to the cavern wall behind you.

The spydr has nine long, powerful legs that could easily step across the chasm, and its body looks like it could support your weight. If the creature is intelligent, you might be able to persuade it to carry you to the next tunnel.

To cross to the other side of the chasm and reach the next tunnel, choose to communicate with the giant spydr, run and jump (with or without Power), or scale the ceiling.

To communicate with the giant spydr: Roll the 20-dice to tell the spydr you wish to leave the cave without a fight. If communication is one of your talents, your roll# + your knowledge# + your skill# + is your adventure#. If communication is not one of your talents, your roll# + your charm# + 1 is your adventure#.

If your adventure# is equal to or more than 15, add the difference to your AP total. The immense spydr is fascinated by your ability to communicate. The intelligent creature is happy to help. You climb on the spydr's back, and it carries you over to the other side of the chasm. Leaving the spydr behind, you may proceed.

If your adventure# is less than 15, subtract the difference from your AP total. The spydr studies you but it does not respond in any way. Still, there's something in its gaze that makes you think the creature is more intelligent than it appears. To make a second attempt to communicate with the giant spydr, roll the 20-dice again for your new roll#. If communication is one of your talents, your new roll# + your knowledge# + your skill# + 1 is your new adventure#. If communication is not one of your talents, your new roll# + your charm# + 2 is your new adventure#.

> *If your new adventure# is equal to or more than 14*, add the difference to your AP total. The spydr allows you to climb on its back, then it steps over the chasm and lets you off in front of the next tunnel. You may proceed.

> *If your new adventure# is less than 14*, subtract the difference from your AP total. If the giant spydr understands you, it doesn't seem to care. The spydr does not budge

from the wall. Proceed to run and jump (below) or scale the ceiling (next page).

To run and jump (without Power): Roll the 10-dice to sprint for the ledge and leap over the chasm. Your roll# + your strength# + 2 is your adventure#.

If your adventure# is equal to or more than 12, add the difference to your AP total. The moment your right foot kicks off from the ledge, your arms and legs pump through the air until you land on the other side of the chasm. You may proceed.

If your adventure# is less than 12, subtract the difference from your AP total. You are uncertain that the ground on the other side is strong enough to support your landing, so you stop short at the edge of the chasm. Proceed to scale the ceiling (next page).

To run and jump (using Power)*: Choose your Jump Power. Roll the 10-dice to sprint for the ledge and leap over the chasm. Your roll# + your Power# + your Power's low-resist# + your strength# is your adventure#.

If your adventure# is equal to or more than 9, add the difference to your AP total. You fly through the air and you land on the other side of the chasm. You may proceed.

If your adventure# is less than 9, subtract the difference from your AP total. You are uncertain that the ground on the other side is strong enough to support your landing, so you stop short at the edge of the chasm. Proceed to scale the ceiling (below).

*NOTE: This counts as one of three Power uses you are allowed on this adventure.

To scale the ceiling: Roll the 20-dice to use the stalactites as handholds to reach the other side of the chasm. Your roll# + your stealth# + your strength# is your adventure#.

If your adventure# is equal to or more than 15, add the difference to your AP total. Gripping one stalactite after the next, you swing hand-over-hand across the ceiling. You arrive at the other side of the chasm, and drop down on the ledge in front of the next cave. You may proceed.

If your adventure# is less than 15, subtract the difference from your AP total. You are halfway over the chasm when the giant spydr scurries up the wall and pursues you across the vaulted ceiling. The spydr's mouth opens and closes, revealing many rows of sharp teeth. It wants you for dinner! If you let go of the stalactites, you will fall and perish in the chasm. You must fight the spydr. To defeat the spydr and reach the other side of the chasm, roll the 20-dice again for your new roll#. Your new roll# + your skill# + your strength# + 1 is your new adventure#.

If your new adventure# is equal to or more than 15, add the difference to your AP total. You kick the spydr. The creature loses its grips on the ceiling and falls down into the chasm. You reach the next cave, and you may proceed.

If your new adventure# is less than 15, subtract the difference from your AP total. The giant spydr avoids your attack. Go back to "roll the 20-dice again for your new roll#" and repeat.

The next cave leads directly to a flight of smooth stone steps. The steps are coated with a thin layer of moist slime, the result of condensation from the cavern. As you carefully climb the slick stones, you see an open doorway at the top of the flight.

A burned-out glow rod extends from an iron bar over the doorway. From where you are standing on the stairs, it looks like the doorway leads to a chamber that is illuminated by a flickering red light. The doorway might lead to a way for you to reenter the fortress. You crouch down at the top of the slime-covered steps and peer into the chamber.

The room contains a circular pool built into the floor. The pool is approximately three meters in diameter, and it's filled with a hot, bubbling fluid. Steam rises from it and carries the scent of chemical waste.

Next to the pool, a thick-link chain is wrapped around a winch mechanism that leads to a pulley secured to the ceiling. At the end of the chain, a hook is secured to a set of metal fetters that grip a green-skinned female alien by her ankles. Hanging upside down over the pool, she is tied up with rope. She has the reptilian skin and facial structure of a Falleen. Her head dangles a mere meter above the bubbling pool, and her eyes are wide with horror.

Beside the pool, a standing Bartokk faces the helpless Falleen. You recognize the Bartokk as the same one who sent you and your ally to the dungeon. The Bartokk still wears the vocabulator around his neck, and in his upper right arm he now wields the confiscated lightsaber. It is the weapon's glow that fills the room with a flickering luminescence, and its hum reverberates in the air. The Bartokk does not appear to be carrying any other weapons, but you do see a restraining bolt activator secured to his belt.

The Bartokk raises the lightsaber, bringing it dangerously close to the chain that keeps the Falleen from falling into the bubbling pool. "The secrets of our mission will die with you," the Bartokk threatens his victim.

Since you need to learn about the Bartokks' mission, you decide to rescue the Falleen. First, you must retrieve the lightsaber and restraining bolt activator from the Bartokk. You slip through the doorway and enter the chamber.

To take the lightsaber and restraining bolt activator away from the Bartokk, choose to use Power or attack the Bartokk.

To take the lightsaber and restraining bolt activator (using Power): Choose your Object Movement Power. Roll the 20-dice to either make the Bartokk relinquish the lightsaber and restraining bolt activator or make the weapon and device fly away from him. Your roll# + your Power# + your Power's low-resist# is your adventure#.

If your adventure# is equal to or more than 13, add the difference to your AP total. The lightsaber and restraining bolt activator are now in your grasp. You may proceed.

If your adventure# is less than 13, subtract the difference from your AP total. You are unable to focus your Power. Proceed to attack the Bartokk (below).

*NOTE: This counts as one of three Power uses you are allowed on this adventure.

To attack the Bartokk: Roll the 10-dice to use the sides of your hands to chop at the Bartokk's shoulders. If maneuvering is one of your talents, your roll# + your strength# + your stealth# + 1 is your adventure#. If maneuvering is not one of your talents, your roll# + your stealth# + your strength# is your adventure#.

If your adventure# is equal to or more than 9, add the difference to your AP total. You strike nerve clusters in the Bartokk's shoulders, forcing him to let go of the lightsaber. You catch the lightsaber and grab the restraining bolt activator from his belt. You may proceed.

If your adventure# is less than 9, subtract 5 AP from your AP total. You did not strike the Bartokk hard enough, and he still grips the lightsaber. To snatch the lightsaber from his claw, roll the 10-dice again for your new roll#. If maneuvering is one of your talents, your new roll# + your strength# + 2 is your new adventure#. If maneuvering is not one of your talents, your new roll# + your strength# + 1 is your new adventure#.

If your new adventure# is equal to or more than 8, add 2 AP to your AP total. Taking care not to touch the lightsaber's deadly beam, you seize the weapon from the Bartokk's claw and the restraining bolt activator from his belt. You may proceed.

If your new adventure# is less than 8, subtract the difference from your AP total. Go back to "roll the 10-dice again for your new roll#" and repeat. When you have taken the lightsaber from the Bartokk, you may proceed.

Now weaponless, the Bartokk takes a cautious step away from you, closer to the bubbling pool over which the bound Falleen continues to struggle.

NOTE: You have retrieved the lightsaber and the restraining bolt activator from the Bartokk. You may now use any of your devices.

Suddenly, two more Bartokks drop down from a hiding place above the doorway. The two Bartokks wield sharp spears.

The vocabulator-equipped Bartokk chitters, then says, "You forget that we Bartokks communicate telepathically. Before your four escorts perished in the dungeon, one of them alerted us of your escape. We knew if you survived the dangers in the cavern, you would eventually enter here." The Bartokk extends a claw toward the Falleen and adds, "We produced this image to make certain we would lure you into this chamber."

As the Bartokk gestures with his claw, the Falleen wavers, fades, then vanishes into thin air, leaving the chain and hook dangling over the pool. The tied-up alien had been a holographic projection. Nothing more than a trick.

You don't like being tricked.

The three Bartokks have earned your wrath. First, you will combat the two Bartokks who carry spears. Choose to fight both spear-wielding Bartokks at once or one at a time.

To fight both spear-wielding Bartokks at once : Roll the 20-dice to run for the open doorway that leads to the slime-covered stone steps. If evasion is one of your talents, your roll# + your stealth# + your strength# +2 is your adventure#. If evasion is not one of your talents, your roll# + your stealth# + your strength# is your adventure#.

If your adventure# is equal to or more than 14, add the difference + 8 to your AP total. As you pass under the doorway, you reach up for the iron bar that supports the burnt-out glow rod. You grab the bar and pull yourself up. The two Bartokks follow you through the doorway at a quick pace, but they make the mistake of stepping on the slime-covered steps. The two Bartokks go sliding down the stairs and fall into the chasm. You may proceed.

If your adventure# is less than 14, subtract the difference from your AP total. The two Bartokks don't pursue you through the doorway. You swing back down into the chamber. Proceed to fight one spear-wielding Bartokk at a time (next page).

To fight one spear-wielding Bartokk at a time: Choose your weapon. Roll the 10-dice to attack the nearest Bartokk. Your roll# + your weaponry# + your weapon's close-range# is your adventure#.

If your adventure# is equal to or more than 9, add the difference + 7 to your AP total. One Bartokk is defeated, and he tumbles to the floor. Go back to "Roll the 10-dice to attack" and repeat. When you have defeated both spear-wielding Bartokks, you may proceed.

If your adventure# is less than 9, subtract 5 AP from your AP total. You only injured the Bartokk, and now the assassin prepares to skewer you with his spear. To resume your attack, roll the 10-dice again for your new roll#. Your new roll# + your weaponry# + your weapon's close-range# + 1 is your new adventure#.

If your new adventure# is equal to or more than 9, add the difference to your AP total. The injured Bartokk is felled. If one spear-wielding Bartokk remains, go back to "roll the 10-dice again for your new roll#" and repeat. After both spear-wielding Bartokks are defeated, you may proceed.

If your new adventure# is less than 9, subtract the difference from your AP total. The

Bartokk nearly slashes you with the tip of his spear. He is putting up an incredible fight, and he moves in for the kill. Go back to "roll the 10-dice again for your new roll#" and repeat. When the two spear-wielding Bartokks are eliminated, you may proceed.

The vocabulator-equipped Bartokk picks up a fallen spear from the floor, then prepares to attack you. If you are going to get any information from the Bartokk, you must take him alive.

Out of the corner of one eye, you notice the metal hook swinging back and forth at the end of the chain that dangles from the ceiling. Below the hook, the toxic pool continues to bubble and steam.

You must subdue the Bartokk. Choose to snag the Bartokk with the hook, fight the Bartokk with a weapon, or fight the Bartokk with your bare hands.

To snag the Bartokk with the hook: Roll the 20-dice to use the winch to lower the chain. If targeting is one of your talents, your roll# + your skill# + 2 is your adventure#. If targeting is not one of your talents, your roll# + your skill# is your adventure#.

If your adventure# is equal to or more than 11, add the difference + 10 to your AP total. You pivot the winch as you lower the chain, and the hook catches the Bartokk. You raise the chain, and the Bartokk dangles helplessly. You may proceed.

If your adventure# is less than 11, subtract the difference from your AP total. The hook misses the Bartokk, but you crank the winch and the hook swings back toward the assassin. For one more chance to snag him with the hook, roll the 20-dice again for your new roll#. Your new roll# + your skill# + 1 is your new adventure#.

> *If your new adventure# is equal to or more than 11*, add the difference to your AP total. The hook catches the Bartokk, and you crank the winch to raise him over the bubbling pool. The Bartokk is helpless, and you may proceed.

> *If your new adventure# is less than 11*, subtract the difference from your AP total. The Bartokk dodges the chain. Now you'll have to fight (below).

To fight the Bartokk with a weapon: Choose your weapon. Roll the 10-dice to stun the Bartokk. Your roll# + your weaponry# +

your weapon's close-range# + 1 is your adventure#.

If your adventure# is equal to or more than 9, add the difference + 5 to your AP total. Despite the Bartokk's ferocious fighting ability, you easily defeat him. The Bartokk is caught. You may proceed.

If your adventure# is less than 9, subtract the difference from your AP total. The Bartokk smashes your weapon from your hand. Proceed to fight the Bartokk with your bare hands (below).

To fight the Bartokk with your bare hands: Roll the 20-dice to teach the Bartokk a lesson in martial arts that he'll never forget. If maneuvering is one of your talents, your roll# + your knowledge# + your strength# is your adventure#. If maneuvering is not one of your talents, your roll# + your strength# is your adventure#.

If your adventure# is equal to or more than 13, add the difference + 7 to your AP total. The armor-plated Bartokk is defeated. You drag him over to the toxic pool so that he can feel the rising steam on the back of his insectoid skull. You may proceed.

If your adventure# is less than 13, subtract 8 AP from your AP total. The Bartokk matches you blow for blow. To execute a quick series of powerful kicks, roll the 20-dice again for your new roll#. If maneuvering is one of your talents, your new roll# + your knowledge# + your strength# + 1 is your new adventure#. If maneuvering is not one of your talents, your new roll# + your strength# + 1 is your new adventure#.

If your new adventure# is equal to or more than 13, add the difference to your AP total. The Bartokk falls to the floor at the edge of the toxic pool. You may proceed.

If your new adventure# is less than 13, subtract the difference from your AP total. The Bartokk is still in a fighting mood. Go back to "roll the 20-dice again for your new roll#" and repeat.

You glare at the vocabulator-equipped Bartokk and state, "You're going to answer some questions."

"You won't get a word out of me," the Bartokk replies in a gravelly voice.

Darth Sidious wants to know the identity of the Bartokks' client and why they stole the Trade Federation droid starfighters from Esseles. You still have the container that you took from the interrogation droid. It holds a full dose of Bavo Six, a truth serum.

You must make the Bartokk answer your questions. Choose to use a mind trick on the Bartokk using Power, frighten the Bartokk, or introduce the truth serum into the Bartokk's system.

To use a mind trick on the Bartokk (using Power)*: Choose your Mind Trick Power. (NOTE: You must be a Jedi or a Sith Lord in order to use this Power). Roll the 20-dice to compel the Bartokk to answer your questions. Your roll# + your Power# + your Power's mid-resist# is your adventure#.

If your adventure# is equal to or more than 13, add the difference + 7 to your AP total. The Bartokk's bulbous black eyes seem to widen, then he agrees to answer your questions. You may proceed.

If your adventure# is less than 13, subtract the difference from your AP total. Despite his battered body, the Bartokk's mind is sharp as ever and he resists your Power. Proceed to frighten the Bartokk (next page) or use the truth serum (next page).

*NOTE: This counts as one of three Power uses you are allowed on this adventure.

To frighten the Bartokk: Roll the 10-dice to threaten that you will drop him into the toxic pool. You must communicate this clearly, or the Bartokk will not believe you are serious. If communication is one of your talents, your roll# + your knowledge# + your charm# is your adventure#. If communication is not one of your talents, your roll# + your charm# is your adventure#.

If your adventure# is equal to or more than 7, add the difference + 6 to your AP total. The shattered Bartokk is uncertain whether he could survive in the bubbling pool, and he agrees to answer your questions. You may proceed.

If your adventure# is less than 7, subtract the difference from your AP total. The Bartokk chitters and nearly convulses in laughter at your threat. He is not afraid of anything, even death. Proceed to use the truth serum (below).

To use truth serum: Roll the 10-dice to use the serum you took from the interrogation droid. Your roll# + your skill# + your knowledge# is your adventure#.

If your adventure# is equal to or more than 9, add the difference + 7 to your AP total. After you give the serum to the Bartokk, his defenses relax and he agrees to tell you whatever you want to know. You may proceed.

If your adventure# is less than 9, subtract 4 AP from your AP total. The Bartokk fights the truth serum. To increase the dose of Bavo Six, roll the 10-dice again for your new roll#. Your new roll# + your skill# + 1 is your new adventure#.

> *If your new adventure# is equal to or more than 7,* add the difference to your AP total. The truth serum works its magic, and the wounded Bartokk agrees to answer all your questions. You may proceed.

> *If your new adventure# is less than 7,* subtract the difference from your AP total. The Bartokk has an incredibly high level of resistance to truth serum. Go back to "roll the 10-dice again for your new roll#" and repeat. When the Bartokk agrees to answer your questions, you may proceed.

Staring at the Bartokk, you demand, "I want to know the name of your client and why you stole the Trade Federation droid starfighters."

Reluctantly, the Bartokk answers, "We were hired by Groodo the Hutt. He owns a factory on Esseles that specializes in the manufacture of customized hyperdrive engines. Our job was to destroy Corulag Academy, but to make it look like the Trade Federation was responsible."

The Bartokk's answer prompts you to ask more questions. "Why did Groodo want to blame the Trade Federation, and how did he know the droid starfighters were on Esseles?"

"The Trade Federation had secretly commissioned Groodo to construct a prototype hyperdrive engine, but they refused to pay him," the Bartokk replies. "Groodo placed a sensor tag on the prototype. He tracked the sensor tag to Trinkatta Starships, where he discovered Trinkatta was constructing fifty droid starfighters. The Hutt hired us to steal the prototype engine as well as the starfighters."

"I saw only twenty-five droid starfighters in the landing bay," you comment. "Where are the other twenty-five and the prototype hyperdrive engine now?"

"They were in another freighter," the Bartokk answers. "It was overtaken by the Jedi."

The Jedi. You are not surprised that they are involved. You can think of only two more questions. "Why does Groodo want to destroy Corulag Academy, and where is he now?"

The Bartokk hesitates, then answers. "Groodo was angered that his son was denied admission to the Academy. Both Groodo and his son are now on their private cruiser, in orbit of Corulag. Groodo wants to watch the destruction of the Academy."

You must admit that Groodo's plan is cunning. By using the droid starfighters to blame the Trade Federation for an attack on Corulag Academy, the Hutt will have his revenge on both the unscrupulous Trade Federation and the discriminating Academy.

Without warning, one of the Bartokk's arms reaches for a concealed weapon. It seems the Bartokk wasn't entirely help-less after all. The weapon is a razor-edged boomerang. He draws his arm back and prepares to throw the boomerang at you.

As the Bartokk readies to throw the boomerang, choose to plunge the Bartokk into the toxic pool (with or without Power), use a weapon to deflect the boomerang, or dodge its razor edges.

To plunge the Bartokk into the toxic pool (using Power)*: Choose your Confusion Power. Roll the 10-dice to confuse the Bartokk into falling back. Your roll# + your stealth# + your Power# + your Power's mid-resist# is your adventure#.

If your adventure# is equal to or more than 8, add the difference + 4 to your AP total. Before the Bartokk can throw the boomerang, he splashes into the pool and his entire body rapidly melts. You may proceed.

If your adventure# is less than 8, subtract the difference from your AP total. The Bartokk is not deceived. He throws the razor-edged boomerang at you. Proceed to use a weapon to deflect the boomerang (next page) or dodge it (page 52).

*NOTE: This counts as one of three Power uses you are allowed on this adventure.

To plunge the Bartokk into the toxic pool (without Power): Roll the 10-dice to either push the Bartokk or hit the winch to lower the chain. Your roll# + your stealth# + your strength# is your adventure#.

If your adventure# is equal to or more than 8, add the difference + 4 to your AP total. Before the Bartokk can throw the boomerang, he splashes into the pool and his entire body rapidly melts. You may proceed.

If your adventure# is less than 8, subtract the difference from your AP total. Either the winch is jammed or the Bartokk resists your push. The Bartokk throws the razor-edged boomerang at you. Proceed to use a weapon to deflect the boomerang (below) or dodge it (next page).

To deflect the boomerang: Choose your weapon. Roll the 20-dice to target the boomerang. If targeting is one of your talents, your roll# + your weaponry# + your weapon's mid-range# + 1 is your adventure#. If targeting is not one of your talents, your roll# + your weaponry# + your weapon's mid-range# is your adventure#.

If your adventure# is equal to or more than 15, add the difference + 5 to your AP total. You strike the boomerang and send it hurtling straight back at the Bartokk. He tries to move away and falls into the deadly pool. You may proceed.

If your adventure# is less than 15, subtract the difference from your AP total. You miss the boomerang, and it's speeding straight at your head. Proceed to dodge the boomerang (below).

To dodge the boomerang: Roll the 20-dice to duck away from the Bartokk's boomerang. If evasion is one of your talents, your roll# + your stealth# + 2 is your adventure#. If evasion is not one of your talents, your roll# + your stealth# is your adventure#.

If your adventure# is equal to or more than 11, add the difference + 4 to your AP total. The boomerang misses you by millimeters, then curves back in midair and returns to the Bartokk. He tries to move away and falls into the deadly pool. You may proceed.

If your adventure# is less than 11, subtract the difference from your AP total. The boomerang spins past your head, then turns in midair. It's angling back at you! Go back to "Roll the 20-

dice to duck away" and repeat. When you have avoided the boomerang and the weapon returns to its doomed owner, you may proceed.

The Bartokk is no longer a threat. Lightsaber in hand, you move forward.

You have gained valuable information about the assassins' assignment. Add 75 AP to your AP total.

At the other end of the chamber, a narrow doorway leads to a circular staircase. You move cautiously up the stairs, wrapping around a central stone column until you reach a large room on the first floor level of the fortress. The room is piled high with explosives and assorted munitions.

Among the many weapons stacked within the room, a plastic box filled with thermal detonators catches your eye. The detonators are shaped like small metal balls and resemble standard grenades, but they contain a powerful synthetic explosive called baradium.

It occurs to you that if you were to set the timer on a single detonator and leave it in the volatile munitions room, the destruction of so many baradium-filled weapons will cause an explosion that might bring down the entire fortress. Since the detonator's timer offers a maximum countdown of ten minutes, you'll have to leave the fortress fast.

There's only one setback. Your ally might still be trapped within the fortress's dungeon. If your ally hasn't escaped by now, there will be little chance for survival.

You decide to set the timer on a thermal detonator and leave it in the munitions room.

To set the timer on the thermal detonator: Roll the 10-dice to enter a ten-minute countdown. Your roll# + your knowledge# + your skill# is your adventure#.

If your adventure# is equal to or more than 9, add the difference to your AP total. You have properly set the timer, and you place the activated thermal detonator back into the plastic box. You may proceed.

If your adventure# is less than 9, subtract 5 AP from your AP total. You accidentally set the timer at ten *seconds*! To reset the timer, roll the 10-dice again for your new roll#. Your new roll# + your knowledge# + your skill# +1 is your new adventure#.

If your new adventure# is equal to or more than 11, add the difference to your AP total. The thermal detonator is properly reset for a ten-minute countdown. You may proceed.

If your new adventure# is less than 11, subtract the difference from your AP total. You didn't have time to reset the detonator, so you had to deactivate it. Go back to "Roll the 10-dice to enter a ten-minute countdown" and repeat. When the timer is correctly set for a ten-minute countdown, you may proceed.

As you place the thermal detonator back in the plastic box, you remove a second detonator and stow it with your other weapons. You don't know whether you'll need a thermal detonator, but you'd rather be prepared.

You leave the munitions room and quickly find your way through the fortress until you reach the courtyard. There, under the light of Ralltiir's moons, the spike-covered Bartokk freighter remains on the landing pad. The freighter's main cargo door is still wide open.

Just beyond the freighter, you see two Bartokks standing beside their repulsorlift skiff. They have retrieved your speeder, and are unloading it from the skiff. You consider making a break for the speeder, but you need to find out what happened to the droid starfighters.

You walk around the freighter to learn the droid starfighters are gone. The six-winged Bartokk starfighter that had been docked to the freighter is also missing. Since the Trade Federation droid starfighters require a central droid control computer to direct their maneuvers, it seems likely that the Bartokk starfighter is carrying the control computer and guiding the fighters to Corulag. The six-winged starfighter carries a crew of three Bartokks for operation, so you are left with at least five Bartokks on Ralltiir.

The departed starfighters were all engineered for hyperspeed. The Bartokk freighter is not capable of traveling through hyperspace. If you are going to pursue the droid starfighters to Corulag, you must return to your starship.

But before you leave, you want to board the freighter and take the Bartokks' tracking sensor technology. If you can secure the technology, you should be able to figure out a way to prevent the Bartokks from tracking your starship when it's in cloak mode.

You consult your chronometer. You have less than six minutes before the thermal detonator explodes in the fortress. Still, obtaining the Bartokks' tracking sensor data is worth the risk.

Over by the skiff, the two Bartokks are examining your speeder. While they are preoccupied, you slip up the freighter's landing ramp and enter the main cargo hold.

You run through a murky corridor until you locate the freighter's bridge. Like everything else on the freighter, the main computer console is designed to be operated by Bartokk claws. However, you are skilled at retrieving information from alien technology. You inspect the scanners and your fingers dart over the controls.

You can download the Bartokks' tracking sensor specifications onto a single data card.

To download the Bartokks' tracking sensor data: Roll the 10-dice to download the specifications. Your roll# + your skill# is your adventure#.

If your adventure# is equal to or more than 8, add a bonus of 150 AP to your AP total. You have obtained information that will render your starship invisible to Bartokk scanners. You may proceed.

If your adventure# is less than 8, subtract 10 AP from your AP total. You entered the wrong commands for downloading. To reenter the correct commands, roll the 10-dice again for your new roll#. Your new roll# + your skill# + 1 is your new adventure#.

If your new adventure# is equal to or more than 10, add a bonus of 150 AP to your AP total. You punch up the data card with the Bartokks' sensor information. Properly used, this data will enable your starship to use its cloaking device to evade Bartokk scanners. You may proceed.

If your new adventure# is less than 10, subtract 10 AP from your AP total. The Bartokks must have put a security lock on their freighter's computer. Unfortunately, the thermal detonator will soon explode, and you don't have time to try another download. You may proceed.

You turn away from the computer console and find yourself facing a Bartokk. The assassin had been sneaking up behind you. In each of his four claws, the Bartokk wields a vibro-ax.

The thermal detonator that you left in the munitions room will blow up in three minutes. Even the freighter might not be safe from the explosion.

You must get off the freighter. Choose to activate the freighter's thrusters, push the Bartokk aside, or combat the Bartokk with a weapon.

To activate the freighter's thrusters: Roll the 10-dice to reach out and punch the thruster controls. Your roll# + your skill# is your adventure#.

If your adventure# is equal to or more than 7, add the difference + 5 to your AP total. The thrusters activate and the entire freighter shudders, knocking the Bartokk off balance.

He falls down upon his own weapons and is defeated. You may proceed.

If your adventure# is less than 7, subtract the difference from your AP total. You pushed the wrong switch, and the Bartokk advances. Proceed to push the Bartokk aside (below) or combat him with a weapon (below).

To push the Bartokk aside: Roll the 10-dice to race by the Bartokk. If maneuvering is one of your talents, your roll# + your strength# + 1 is your adventure#. If maneuvering is not one of your talents, your roll# + your strength# is your adventure#.

If your adventure# is equal to or more than 8, add the difference + 4 to your AP total. You push the Bartokk so hard that he smashes into an open instrument panel. The Bartokk is stunned, and you may proceed.

If your adventure# is less than 8, subtract the difference from your AP total. The agile Bartokk dodges your maneuver and blocks your exit. Proceed to combat the Bartokk with a weapon (below).

To combat the Bartokk with a weapon: Choose your weapon. Roll the 20-dice to target the vibro-ax wielding Bartokk. If targeting is one of your talents, your roll# + your weaponry# + your weapon's mid-range# + 1 is your adventure#. If targeting is not one of your talents, your roll# + your weaponry# + your weapon's mid-range# is your adventure#.

If your adventure# is equal to or more than 15, add the difference to your AP total. The Bartokk is no match for your skill. He crashes to the floor, and you may proceed.

If your adventure# is less than 15, subtract 7 AP from your AP total. The Bartokk swings the four vibro-axes in an unpredictable fashion until he forces you back into a corner. To lash back at the vibro-ax-wielding Bartokk, roll the 20-dice again for your new roll#. Your new roll# + your weaponry# + your weapon's close-range# + 1 is your new adventure#.

If your new adventure# is equal to or more than 15, add the difference to your AP total. Fighting your way out of the corner, you defeat the Bartokk. You may proceed.

If your new adventure# is less than 15, subtract 8 AP from your AP total. You have rendered the Bartokk unconscious, but he topples toward you with his vibro-axes still buzzing away. If he lands on you, you're done for. To jump away from the falling

Bartokk, roll the 20-dice again for your new roll#. If evasion is one of your talents, your new roll# + your stealth# +1 is your new adventure#. If evasion is not one of your talents, your new roll# + your stealth# is your new adventure#.

If your new adventure# is equal to or more than 12, add the difference to your AP total. You jump away as the Bartokk collapses into the corner, landing on his own weapons. You may proceed.

If your new adventure# is less than 12, subtract the difference from your AP total. You jump away in time, but the Bartokk was only pretending to be unconscious! He renews his efforts to cut you down. Go back to "roll the 20-dice again for your new roll#" and repeat. When you have defeated the Bartokk, you may proceed.

You check your chronometer as you run down the murky corridor to the freighter's main cargo hold. You now have less than a minute to escape the fortress compound before the thermal detonator explodes.

You race down the freighter's landing

ramp and head straight for your speeder. The two Bartokks are still so busy examining it that they don't see you running toward them. They stumble back in surprise as you leap onto your speeder.

To speed out of the courtyard: Choose your vehicle (it must be capable of traveling over land). Roll the 10-dice to initiate your vehicle's thrusters. Your roll# + your vehicle's speed# + 2 is your adventure#.

If your adventure# is equal to or more than 8, add the difference + 10 to your AP total. You tear away from the surprised Bartokks and their skiff. Your vehicle shoots up and out of the fortress's landing bay, and you may proceed.

If your adventure# is less than 8, subtract the difference from your AP total. The lousy Bartokks have readjusted your vehicle's operating controls. To quickly reset the controls, roll the 10-dice again for your new roll#. Your new roll# + your knowledge# + your skill# + 1 is your new adventure#.

If your new adventure# is equal to or more than 9, add the difference to your AP total. The controls are now properly adjusted. Go back to "Roll the 10-dice to initiate your vehicle's thrusters" and repeat. After you have left the two Bartokks in your dust, you may proceed.

If your new adventure# is less than 9, subtract the difference from your AP total. Your vehicle's controls are still not responding. Go back to "roll the 10-dice again for your new roll#" and repeat. When you have reset the controls and blasted away from the two Bartokks, you may proceed.

As you zoom away from the fortress, you quickly check your chronometer. In your head, you count off the final seconds.

Five . . . four . . . three . . . two . . .

Behind you, the entire fortress is instantly wracked by a massive, thunderous explosion as the thermal detonator blows up in the munitions room. You look back over your shoulder to see the fortress lit up like daylight by the incredible blast. Raging fires sweep up the three silo-like towers, then one of the towers buckles and falls, smashing down on the Bartokk freighter. Although you worry about the fate of your ally, you find the sound of the freighter's rupturing hull to be most satisfying.

Suddenly, a blaster bolt strikes your vehicle. Turning your head to cast a glance over your other shoulder and see you are being pursued across the sky by the two Bartokks on their repulsorlift skiff.

As impossible as it is to conceive, they escaped the explosion.

Both Bartokks grip a set of skiff controls with their lower arms while their upper arms carry bowcasters. The blaster bolt came from one assassin's bowcaster. He is preparing to fire another blaster bolt.

Before you can return to your starship, you'll have to outmaneuver the Bartokks on their flying skiff. Choose to evade the skiff, ram the skiff, throw the thermal detonator at the Bartokks, or combat the Bartokks with a weapon. You only have one thermal detonator, so if you throw it, you won't be able to use it again.

To evade the skiff: Roll the 10-dice to fly your vehicle back toward the burning fortress. Your roll# + your vehicle's speed# + your vehicle's stealth# is your adventure#.

If your adventure# is equal to or more than 8, add the difference + 6 to your AP total. You fly by one of the fortress's flaming towers. As you near the tower, you pull up fast. The Bartokks follow you but they don't pull up fast enough. The skiff smashes into the flaming tower, and you may proceed.

If your adventure# is less than 8, subtract the difference from your AP total. The Bartokks' skiff stays tight on your vehicle's tail as you fly low over the burning fortress. One of the other silo-like towers looks like it's going to topple. To fly dangerously close to the tower, roll the 10-dice again for your new roll#. Your new roll# + your navigation# + your vehicle's speed# is your new adventure#.

If your new adventure# is equal to or more than 8, add the difference to your AP total. Just as you fly past the tower, the structure begins to fall. Before your Bartokk pursuers can pull away, the building topples down on their skiff. You may proceed.

If your new adventure# is less than 8, subtract the difference from your AP total. You are unable to shake the Bartokk skiff. Proceed to ram the skiff (next page), throw the thermal detonator (next page) or combat the Bartokks with a weapon (page 69).

To ram the skiff: Roll the 20-dice to loop back on a collision course for the Bartokk skiff. Your roll# + your navigation + your vehicle's stealth# is your adventure#.

If your adventure# is equal to or more than 13, add the difference + 5 to your AP total. Flying over the canyon, your reinforced vehicle slams into the side of the Bartokk skiff. The two Bartokks lose their grips and are thrown from their craft. They are not wearing parachutes, and it's a long, long way down to the rocky canyon floor. Your vehicle holds up fine, and you may proceed.

If your adventure# is less than 13, subtract the difference from your AP total. The Bartokks swiftly maneuver their skiff away from your reckless ramming attempt. Proceed to throw the thermal detonator (below), or combat the Bartokks with a weapon (page 69).

To throw the thermal detonator at the Bartokks: Roll the 10-dice to slide the explosive device's thumb trigger and lob it at the flying skiff. If targeting is one of your talents, your roll# + your strength# + 2 is your adventure#. If targeting is not one of your talents, your roll# + your strength# is your adventure#.

If your adventure# is equal to or more than 7, add the difference + 7 to your AP total. To the Bartokks' horror, your neatly thrown thermal detonator lands inside their skiff. The detonator explodes, destroying the skiff and its crew. You may proceed.

If your adventure# is less than 7, subtract the difference from your AP total. You throw the thermal detonator straight at the skiff, but one of the Bartokks swings his crossbow hard and bats the detonator back at you. You raise your hand to knock the explosive back at the skiff. Roll the 10-dice again for your new roll#. If maneuvering is one of your talents, your new roll# + your strength# + 2 is your new adventure#. If maneuvering is not one of your talents, your new roll# + your strength# + 1 is your new adventure#.

If your new adventure# is equal to or more than 8, add the difference to your AP total. You knock the explosive device right back at the assassins. The detonator explodes, taking the skiff and the Bartokks with it. You may proceed.

If your new adventure# is less than 8, subtract the difference from your AP total. You knock the thermal detonator back at the Bartokks, but the skiff falls back rapidly.

The detonator explodes in midair and does not destroy anything. The skiff continues to pursue you. Proceed to combat the Bartokks with a weapon (below).

To combat the Bartokks with a weapon: Choose your weapon. Roll the 20-dice to target the skiff's engine housing. If targeting is one of your talents, your roll# + your weaponry# + your weapon's far-range# + 1 is your adventure#. If targeting is not one of your talents, your roll# + your weaponry# + your weapon's far-range# is your adventure#.

If your adventure# is equal to or more than 13, add the difference + 4 to your AP total. The flying skiff's engine explodes, and the two Bartokks go down with their vehicle. You may proceed.

If your adventure# is less than 13, subtract the difference from your AP total. You miss the skiff's engine housing, and the Bartokks draw away from your vehicle. The two assassins prepare to fire their bowcasters at you. You'll have to target each Bartokk, one at a time. To target one of the Bartokks on the skiff, roll the 20-dice again for your new roll#. If targeting is one of your talents, your new roll# + your weaponry# + your weaponry's far-range# + 1 is your new adventure#. If targeting is not one of your talents, your new roll# + your weaponry# + your weaponry's far-range# is your new adventure#.

If your new adventure# is equal to or more than 13, add the difference to your AP total. You have eliminated one Bartokk. To attack the second Bartokk, go back to "roll the 20-dice again for your new roll#" and repeat. When you have defeated both Bartokks, they plummet to the canyon floor in their out-of-control skiff, and you may proceed.

If your new adventure# is less than 13, subtract the difference from your AP total. You missed the Bartokk. Go back to "roll the 20-dice again for your new roll#" and repeat. When both Bartokks are defeated, you may proceed.

You fly your vehicle down to the canyon floor. Your starship is exactly where you left it. As you angle your vehicle toward your starship, you catch sight of a lone Bartokk guard. The Bartokk is standing on the ground near the stern of your starship. From his relaxed stance, you determine he doesn't see your approach.

You cannot allow the Bartokk guard to

prevent you from boarding your starship. Choose to attack the Bartokk guard with your vehicle or with a weapon.

To attack the Bartokk guard with your vehicle: Roll the 10-dice to increase velocity and aim your speeder at the Bartokk guard. Your roll# + your navigation# + your vehicle's speed# is your adventure#.

If your adventure# is equal to or more than 8, add the difference to your AP total. The Bartokk is downed, and you may proceed.

If your adventure# is less than 8, subtract the difference from your AP total. The Bartokk sees your approach! Before you can strike him down, he ducks out of the way. Proceed to combat the Bartokk with your weapon (below).

To attack the Bartokk guard with a weapon: Choose your weapon. Roll the 20-dice to cut down the guard. Your roll# + your weaponry# + your weapon's mid-range# is your adventure#.

If your adventure# is equal to or more than 13, add the difference to your AP total. Your skillful use of weaponry has eliminated yet another opponent. You may proceed.

If your adventure# is less than 13, subtract 10 AP from your AP total. You miss the guard. With dazzling speed, he leaps onto the back of your vehicle and prepares to strike you with his claws. If you use your weapon, you might damage your own vehicle. To throw the Bartokk from your speeding vehicle, roll the 20-dice again for your new roll#. If maneuvering is one of your talents, your new roll# + your strength# + your stealth# + 1 is your new adventure#. If maneuvering is not one of your talents, your new roll# + your strength# + your stealth# is your new adventure#.

If your new adventure# is equal to or more than 15, add the difference to your AP total. You grip the Bartokk by one of his wrists, then hurl him from your vehicle. You may proceed.

If your new adventure# is less than 15, subtract the difference from your AP total. Still on the back of your vehicle, the Bartokk puts up a fight. Go back to "roll the 20-dice again for your new roll#" and repeat. When the guard is hurled to the rocks below, you may proceed.

You land your repulsorlift vehicle next to your starship. At first, it seems the Bartokk guard left your ship untouched. But after you return your vehicle to its storage compartment in the starship's underside cargo hatch, you notice deep scratches on the aft hatchway. Still, the hatch is sealed, so you assume the Bartokks have not been able to breach your ship's security system. You open the aft hatch, enter the starship, and scramble into the bridge.

If the Bartokk starfighter and twenty-five droid starfighters are traveling through hyperspace by way of the Perlemian Trade Route, they're probably halfway to Corulag by now. Your own starship is equipped with a Sienar SSDS 11-A hyperdrive, which is more powerful than any of the Bartokk or Trade Federation droid starfighters. If you leave now, you might actually beat the enemy to the Corulag system. You must launch your starship off of Ralltiir, then make the jump to hyperspace. Proceed to launch your starship.

To launch your starship: Choose your vehicle (it must be capable of space travel). Roll the 20-dice to initiate launch. Your roll# + your skill# + your vehicle's speed# is your adventure#.

If your adventure# is equal to or more than 14, add the difference + 5 to your AP total. Your starship lifts off from the canyon floor and blasts up into the sky. Barely a minute later, your starship leaves Ralltiir's stratosphere and enters space. You may proceed to make the jump to hyperspace (below).

If your adventure# is less than 14, subtract the difference from your AP total. Your starship's repulsorlift engine failed to catch. Perhaps the Bartokks tampered with your starship after all. Go back to "Roll the 20-dice to initiate launch" and repeat.

To make the jump to hyperspace: Roll the 20-dice to set your nav computer for the Corulag system in the Bormea sector and activate your starship's hyperdrive. Your roll# + your skill# + your vehicle's distance# is your adventure#.

If your adventure# is equal to or more than 14, add the difference + 6 to your AP total. Your vessel angles in the direction of Corulag, and the stars appear to elongate away from the central point of your destination. You race through hyperspace, and you may proceed.

If your adventure# is less than 14, subtract 8 AP from your AP total. There's something wrong with your hyperspace motivator. To repair the hyperspace motivator, roll the 20-dice again for your new roll#. Your new roll# + your skill# is your new adventure#.

If your new adventure# is equal to or more than 12, add the difference to your AP total. The hyperspace motivator is fixed. Go back to "Roll the 20-dice to set your nav computer" and repeat. When you have entered hyperspace, you may proceed.

If your new adventure# is less than 12, subtract the difference from your AP total. The hyperspace motivator requires extra fine tuning. Go back to "roll the 20-dice again for your new roll#" and repeat. After you have fixed the motivator and then launched into hyperspace, you may proceed.

As your starship races through hyperspace to the Corulag system, your thoughts turn to your lost ally. The starship's bridge feels empty without him on board.

You glance at a computer monitor to check your starship's functions. On the surface of the monitor's screen, you see the reflection of something moving behind you.

Spinning around in your seat, you face a Bartokk. The assassin managed to infiltrate your ship after all, and must have already been on board when you blasted off of Ralltiir. The Bartokk stowaway stands in front of the aft hatch, clicking his mandibles together as he makes a horrid chittering sound. He bends his lean-muscled legs and prepares to spring at you.

Choose to open the aft hatch, fight the Bartokk using a weapon, or fight the Bartokk with your bare hands.

To open the aft hatch: Roll the 10-dice to grip the console while you punch a switch that will open the aft hatch. Your roll# + your skill# is your adventure#.

If your adventure# is equal to or more than 6, add the difference + 10 to your AP total. The aft hatch snaps open and all the air races out of the bridge. While you cling to the console, the Bartokk is sucked out of the starship and into hyperspace. You quickly press the switch again, and the hatch seals. The bridge repressurizes, and you may proceed.

If your adventure# is less than 6, subtract the difference from your AP total. The aft hatch is stuck and won't open. The Bartokk springs forward across the starship's bridge. Proceed to fight the Bartokk using your weapon (below).

To fight the Bartokk using your weapon:
Roll the 20-dice to fend off the attacking assassin. Your roll# + your weaponry# + your weapon's mid-range# is your adventure#.

If your adventure# is equal to or more than 14, add the difference + 7 to your AP total. You score a direct hit on the Bartokk, and he drops to the floor. You may proceed.

If your adventure# is less than 14, subtract the difference from your AP total. You miss the Bartokk, and he slaps your weapon from your hand. Proceed to fight the Bartokk with your bare hands (below).

To fight the Bartokk with your bare hands: Roll the 20-dice to cut down the Bartokk by using your martial arts skills. If maneuvering is one of your talents, your roll# + your knowledge# + your strength# is your adventure#. If maneuvering is not one of your talents, your roll# + your strength# + 1 is your adventure#.

If your adventure# is equal to or more than 11, add the difference + 3 to your AP total. You unleash your savage fighting techniques on the unprepared Bartokk. It's an easy knockout. You may proceed.

If your adventure# is less than 11, subtract 9 AP from your AP total. Despite your skill at hand-to-hand combat, the Bartokk will not be easily defeated. You must increase your strength. To use more strength to bash the Bartokk, roll the 20-dice again for your new roll#. If maneuvering is one of your talents, your new roll# + your knowledge# + your strength# +2 is your new adventure#. If maneuvering is not one of your talents, your new roll# + your strength# + 2 is your new adventure#.

If your new adventure# is equal to or more than 11, add the difference to your AP total. Finally, you defeat the ferocious Bartokk. You may proceed.

If your new adventure# is less than 11, subtract the difference from your AP total. The Bartokk only fights with greater ferocity. Go back to "roll the 20-dice again for your new roll#" and repeat. After you have defeated the Bartokk, you may proceed.

Still speeding through hyperspace, your starship enters the Corulag system. The nav computer automatically deactivates the starship's hyperdrive, and there's a slight shudder as the vessel reenters real-space.

You conduct a quick sensor scan of the area. There isn't any sign of the Bartokk or droid starfighters. You've managed to beat them to Corulag.

For arriving first, reward yourself by adding 100 AP to your AP total.

Through your viewport, you see the planet, ten thousand kilometers away. Even though Corulag is located on the lucrative Perlemian Trade Route, it does not look like a remarkable world. However, it is home to several billion citizens and the prestigious Corulag Academy. At the Academy, students are trained to become members of the Exploration, Military, and Merchant Services for the Republic.

According to the vocabulator-equipped Bartokk, Groodo the Hutt has hired the assassins to destroy Corulag Academy because his son was denied admission to the institution. The Bartokk also said that

Groodo intended to watch the Academy's destruction from his cruiser.

You activate your sensors and scan the Corulag system for any orbiting vessels besides unmanned satellites. Only one blip appears on your sensor screen.

As you travel toward the orbiting vessel's location, your telescopic sensors produce a magnified visual of a medium-size cruiser. It's decked out with broad fins and large oval viewports, and the hull is painted in vibrant reds and yellows. In your estimation, such an ugly ship could only be owned by a Hutt.

Suddenly, your hyperwave warning light starts pulsating. Twenty-six starfighters are about to exit hyperspace in your proximity. Unless you activate your starship's cloaking device immediately, the starfighters will see you. Proceed to activate your starship's cloaking device.

To activate your starship's cloaking device: Roll the 10-dice to make your ship invisible. Your roll# + your skill# is your adventure#.

If your adventure# is equal to or more than 5, add the difference to your AP total. Your starship's exterior vanishes from view. You may proceed.

If your adventure# is less than 5, subtract the difference from your AP total. Your cloak field generator is low on energy. To channel auxiliary power to the cloak field generator, roll the 10-dice again for your new roll#. Your new roll# + your skill# + 1 is your new adventure#.

If your new adventure# is equal to or more than 10, add 2 AP to your AP total. The cloak field generator kicks in, and your starship is rendered invisible to onlookers. You may proceed.

If your new adventure# is less than 10, subtract the difference from your AP total. Go back to "roll the 10-dice again for your new roll#" and repeat. When you have re-energized the cloak field generator, your starship disappears and you may proceed.

Just as your starship vanishes, twenty-five droid starfighters and a single Bartokk starfighter enter realspace. The fighters zip in fast, then their sublight engines take over and they decelerate to a relatively slow crawl. The droid starfighters are all in flight mode, with their wings retracted to maintain a sleek profile. Flying behind them, the six-winged Bartokk starfighter controls the droids' flight paths. Since the Bartokks take up most of the available space within their starfighter, you assume they must have a compact droid central control computer on board.

You cannot allow the Bartokks to use the Trade Federation droid starfighters to assault Corulag Academy. If the Trade Federation is blamed for an attack on Corulag, it would draw unwanted attention to the Trade Federation in this sector, and possibly affect Darth Sidious's plans for the future.

You are contemplating the best way to defeat the starfighter armada when the Bartokks' ship approaches your position. Since they can't see you, you pull back so they won't collide with your cloaked starship. Their starfighter passes so close to your invisible ship that you can look through their fighter's triangular viewports and see the Bartokk pilot, gunner, and tailgunner seated back-to-back within.

Suddenly, the Bartokks are illuminated by a bright, flashing warning light in the cockpit, and all three assassins turn their insectoid heads to peer out the viewports in your direction. You were so confident in your starship's cloaking device, you forgot about the Bartokks' sophisticated sensors.

They know where you are.

Before you can react, the Bartokk starfighter swings away from your starship, and all twenty-five droid starfighters turn toward you. Despite your ship's invisibility, all the starfighters have locked onto your position. The droid starfighters' wings snap into attack mode, revealing their lethal blaster cannons.

You must get past the droid starfighters to reach the Bartokks. If you successfully retrieved tracking sensor data from the Bartokk freighter on Ralltiir, you can modify your starship's cloaking device to make your ship invisible to the Bartokks' scanners. The data supplied by Darth Sidious will enable your ship's computer to seize control of the droid starfighters. You can also try activating your transmission jammers to disrupt the signal from the Bartokk ship that commands the droid starfighters.

To get past the droid starfighters, choose to modify your starship's cloaking device (you must have successfully retrieved the tracking sensor data from the Bartokk freighter on Ralltiir, on page 58), seize control of the droid starfighters, activate your transmission jammers, or destroy the Bartokk starfighter's main antennae.

To modify your starship's cloaking device: Roll the 10-dice to install the Bartokk sensor data into your computer. You must have received the information on page 58 in order to do this. Your roll# is your adventure#.

If your adventure# is 1 or 2, subtract 20 AP from your AP total. You accidentally erase the Bartokk sensor data. Although your starship is invisible to the naked eye, it still appears on the Bartokks' scanner. Proceed to seize control of the droid starfighters (next page).

If your adventure# is 3 or 4, subtract 5 AP from your AP total. You installed the Bartokk sensor data into the wrong data port. Go back to "Roll the 10-dice to install" and repeat.

If your adventure# is 5 or 6, add 20 AP to your AP total. Your cloaking device is now impervious to Bartokk scanners. The Bartokks don't know how or where to direct the droid starfighters to attack your ship. However, the Bartokks are still in control of the droid starfighters, and they send the droid starfighters on an erratic, weaving course. Unless you do something fast, you might be rammed by one of the fighters. Proceed to activate your transmission jammers (page 87).

If your adventure# is 7 or 8, subtract 10 AP from your AP total. The Bartokk data is incompatible with your starship's computer. You must proceed to seize control of the droid starfighters (below).

If your adventure # is 9 or 10, add 40 AP to your AP total. Your cloaking device is now programmed to evade detection from Bartokk scanners, and the three Bartokks don't know the location of your ship anymore. As an unexpected bonus, the installed data interfaces with your starship's computer, and you can now direct the Trade Federation droid starfighters by remote control. You may proceed.

To seize control of the droid starfighters: Roll the 20-dice to use your starship's computer and broadcast signal to take over the operation of the Trade Federation fighters. Your roll# + your knowledge# + your skill# is your adventure#.

If your adventure# is equal to or more than 14, add the difference + 10 to your AP total. Thanks to the Trade Federation data card supplied by Darth Sidious, you now have complete control over all twenty-five droid starfighters. You may proceed.

If your adventure# is less than 14, subtract the difference from your AP total. The droid starfighters do not respond to your signal. To try entering a different set of command instructions for the droid starfighters, roll the 20-dice again for your new roll#. Your new roll# + your knowledge# + your skill# + 1 is your new adventure#.

If your new adventure# is equal to or more than 14, add the difference to your AP total. You have entered the correct commands into your computer, and you are now able to operate the droid starfighters by remote control. You may proceed.

If your new adventure# is less than 14, subtract the difference from your AP total. You entered the correct sequence, but it will take time for your computer to take complete control of the Trade Federation droid starfighters. Proceed to activate your transmission jammers (next page).

To activate your transmission jam-mers: Roll the 10-dice to disrupt the signal from the Bartokk ship that commands the droid starfighters. Your roll# + your skill# + 2 is your adventure#.

If your adventure# is equal to or more than 8, add the difference + 8 to your AP total. You not only jam the Bartokks' transmission, but your sensors identify the operating frequency for the droid starfighters. Your computer au-tomatically takes control of them, and you may proceed.

If your adventure# is less than 8, subtract the difference from your AP total. You are unable to jam the Bartokks' transmission, and the droid starfighters attack your ship. Proceed to destroy the Bartokk starfighter's main anten-nae (below).

To destroy the Bartokk starfighter's main antennae: Roll the 20-dice to fly away from the droid starfighters and target the Bar-tokk starfighter's antennae array. If targeting is one of your talents, your roll# + your weaponry# + your vehicle's weaponry# +1 is your adven-ture#. If targeting is not one of your talents, your roll# + your weaponry# + your vehicle's weaponry# is your adventure#.

If your adventure# is equal to or more than 14, add the difference + 9 to your AP total. Your starship's laser cannons fire upon the Bartokk starfighter's main antennae, and the entire antennae array blows up. The Bartokks are no longer able to control the droid starfighters, and your cloaked ship has vanished from their sensor screens. Thanks to the data supplied by Darth Sidious, your starship's computer takes control of the droid starfighters. You may proceed.

If your adventure# is less than 14, subtract 7 AP from your AP total. The Bartokk starfighter executes a tight loop and you miss the antennae. The Bartokks come up fast behind your cloaked ship and fire a proton torpedo. To avoid the torpedo, roll the 20-dice again for your new roll#. Your new roll# + your navigation# + your vehicle's stealth# is your new adventure#.

If your new adventure# is equal to or more than 14, add the difference to your AP total. Flying evasively, you manage to avoid the proton torpedo, and the explosive device speeds past your ship before it detonates at a safe distance. Go back to "Roll the 20-dice to fly away" and repeat, but be careful; the Bartokks might fire another torpedo. When you have destroyed the

Bartokk starfighter's antennae, you may proceed.

If your new adventure# is less than 14, subtract the difference from your AP total. You dodge the torpedo — but it boomerangs back to attack again. Go back to "roll the 20-dice again for your new roll#" and repeat. When you have successfully evaded the torpedo and destroyed the Bartokk starfighter's antennae, you may proceed.

You are now in command of all twenty-five Federation droid starfighters, and the Bartokks can no longer detect your cloaked starship.

Add 75 AP to your AP total.

The Bartokks must be eliminated. To destroy the Bartokks, choose to use Power, fire your laser cannons at the Bartokk starfighter, or command the droid starfighters to destroy the Bartokk ship.

To destroy the Bartokk starfighter (using Power)*: Choose your Confusion Power. Roll the 20-dice to make the Bartokks fire a torpedo that will boomerang back at them. Your roll# + your Power# + your Power's mid-resist# is your adventure#.

If your adventure# is equal to or more than 11, add the difference + 12 to your AP total. The Bartokks destroy their own ship, and you may proceed.

If your adventure# is less than 11, subtract the difference from your AP total. The strong-willed Bartokks resist your Power and prepare to fire a proton torpedo at your starship. Proceed to fire your laser cannons at the Bartokk starfighter (below) or command the droid starfighters to attack their ship (page 92).

*NOTE: This counts as one of three Power uses you are allowed on this adventure.

To fire your laser cannons at the Bartokk starfighter: Roll the 20-dice to shoot at the Bartokk's fighter. If targeting is one of your talents, your roll# + your weaponry# + your vehicle's weaponry# + 1 is your adventure#. If targeting is not one of your talents, your roll# + your weaponry# + your vehicle's weaponry# is your adventure#.

If your adventure# is equal to or more than 14, add the difference + 10 to your AP total. You score six direct hits on the Bartokks' starfighter, and the six-winged craft explodes, spraying debris in every direction. You may proceed.

If your adventure# is less than 14, subtract 7 AP from your AP total. The Bartokks avoid your barrage, and fire a concussion missile. Such a missile will produce a shock wave that could penetrate your ship's deflector shields. Although the Bartokks can't see you, they've fired a lucky shot in your general direction. Instead of taking evasive action, you decide to target the oncoming torpedo. To shoot the torpedo, roll the 20-dice again for your new roll#. Your new roll# + your weaponry# + your vehicle's weaponry# +1 is your new adventure#.

> *If your new adventure# is equal to or more than 14*, add the difference to your AP total. You shoot the torpedo, and the resulting explosion destroys both the torpedo and the Bartokk starfighter. The Bartokks are defeated, and you may proceed.

> *If your new adventure# is less than 14*, subtract the difference from your AP total. You only manage to strike one of the concussion missile's four stabilizer fins, knocking it onto a collision course with your starship! You must fly out of its path. To avoid being struck by the proton torpedo, roll the 20-

dice again for your new roll#. Your new roll# + your navigation# + your vehicle's stealth# is your new adventure#.

If your new adventure# is equal to or more than 13, add the difference to your AP total. You outmaneuver the missile, and the lethal projectile speeds past you and explodes in deep space. Now you must go back to "Roll the 20-dice to shoot at the Bartokks' fighter" and repeat. When you have eliminated the Bartokks, you may proceed.

If your new adventure# is less than 13, subtract the difference from your AP total. The concussion missile explodes and knocks out your deflector shields! Although your starship is undamaged, it will take time for your deflector shields to fully recharge. Proceed to command the droid starfighters to destroy the Bartokk ship (below).

To command the droid starfighters to destroy the Bartokk ship: Roll the 10-dice to use your starship's computer to direct the droid starfighters. Your roll# + your navigation# + your skill# is your adventure#.

If your adventure# is equal to or more than 9, add the difference + 10 to your AP total. All twenty-five droid starfighters fire at the Bartokks' ship. The Bartokk starfighter is consumed in a massive explosion, and you may proceed.

If your adventure# is less than 9, subtract the difference from your AP total. Your starship's computer starts to overheat at the strain of trying to control all twenty-five droid starfighters. You decide to try controlling only twelve droid starfighters. To direct twelve droid starfighters in an attack formation, roll the 10-dice again for your new roll#. Your new roll# + your navigation# + your skill# + 1 is your new adventure#.

If your new adventure# is equal to or more than 9, add the difference to your AP total. The twelve droid starfighters fire their blaster cannons and the Bartokk starfighter bursts into fire and smoke. You adjust your starship's computer and are now able to control all twenty-five droid starfighters. The Bartokks are destroyed, and you may proceed.

If your new adventure# is less than 9, subtract the difference from your AP total. You accidentally direct the twelve droid starfighters to fly in the wrong direction. Go back to "roll the 10-dice again for your new roll#" and repeat. When the droid starfighters have blown up the Bartokks' ship, you may proceed.

During your battle with the Bartokks, the red-and-yellow cruiser has remained in orbit of Corulag. Although you aren't certain whether the cruiser belongs to Groodo the Hutt, you decide it's time to find out.

Your ship is in full cloak mode as you leave the twenty-five droid starfighters behind and fly toward the orbital cruiser. When you draw within firing range, you transmit a message to the brightly painted vessel.

"Come in, Groodo," you utter into your ship-to-ship comm unit.

Seconds later, the three-dimensional image of a corpulent Hutt appears from your communication console's holocom projector. Although the image is a bit fuzzy, the Hutt's lower lip is moving from side to side, and his thick cheeks look like they're quite stuffed. It seems you've interrupted the Hutt during a meal.

"What's the meaning of this interruption?" the Hutt snarls.

"There won't be any attack on Corulag Academy," you state.

"What?!" the Hutt sputters. "I mean . . . I don't know what you're talking about!"

"You made a grave error when you ordered the Bartokks to steal from the Trade Federation property," you respond. "Consider this fair warning: You have thirty seconds to evacuate your cruiser before I destroy it."

"You dare threaten the mighty Groodo?" the Hutt retorts. "Show yourself!"

"Twenty seconds," you reply.

"Who *are* you?" the Hutt demands, sounding only slightly annoyed.

You switch off the comm unit.

If you did not use your thermal detonator to attack the two skiff-riding Bartokks on Ralltiir, the explosive device could now come in handy. To destroy the Hutt's cruiser, choose to plant a thermal detonator on the cruiser's main docking hatch (you must still have a thermal detonator), shoot at the cruiser's oval viewports, or command the droid starfighters to attack the cruiser.

To plant a thermal detonator on the cruiser's main docking hatch: Roll the 10-dice to dock your invisible ship to the Hutt's cruiser, then secure the detonator to the cruiser's docking hatch. Your roll# + your stealth# + your vehicle's stealth# is your adventure#.

If your adventure# is equal to or more than 9, add the difference + 20 to your AP total. Leaving the thermal detonator at a setting for a six-second countdown, you pull your starship away from the cruiser. The cruiser's hatch explodes, causing a chain reaction of several more explosions that tear the ship in half. The Hutt's cruiser is destroyed, and you may proceed.

If your adventure# is less than 9, subtract the difference from your AP total. The thermal detonator was a dud. Proceed to shoot at the cruiser's oval viewports (below) or command the droid starfighters to attack (page 98).

To shoot at the cruiser's oval viewports: Roll the 10-dice to aim your laser cannons at the cruiser's viewports. If targeting is one of your talents, your roll# + your weaponry# + your vehicle's weaponry# + 1 is your adventure#. If targeting is one of your talents, your roll# + your weaponry# + your vehicle's weaponry# is your adventure#.

If your adventure# is equal to or more than 10, add the difference + 20 to your AP total. You shoot out the viewports, and air rapidly escapes the Hutt's cruiser. The entire vessel depressurizes and implodes. You may proceed.

If your adventure# is less than 10, subtract 4 AP from your AP total. The hull of the Hutt's cruiser is layered with concealed cluster bombs. As you fire at the cruiser, the cluster bombs' short-range sensors locate your approximate firing position and spray explosive shrapnel at your cloaked ship. To avoid being hit by the explosive shrapnel, roll the 10-dice again for your new roll#. If evasion is one of your talents, your new roll# + your navigation# + your vehicle's stealth# + 1 is your new adventure#. If evasion is not one of your talents, your new roll# + your navigation# + your vehicle's stealth# is your new adventure#.

If your new adventure# is equal to or more than 10, add the difference to your AP total. You steer clear of the cluster bombs' sprayed shrapnel. Go back to "Roll the 10-dice to aim your laser cannons" and repeat. When you have destroyed the Hutt's cruiser, you may proceed.

If your new adventure# is less than 10, subtract the difference from your AP total. The explosive shrapnel weakens your deflector shields. Proceed to command the droid starfighters to attack the cruiser (below).

To command the droid starfighters to attack the cruiser: Roll the 20-dice to call all twenty-five droid starfighters and direct them to fire their blaster cannons at the Hutt's brightly painted cruiser. Your roll# + your navigation# + your skill# is your adventure#.

If your adventure# is equal to or more than 13, add the difference + 20 to your AP total. Although the Hutt's cruiser has powerful deflector shields, they buckle and fail under the assault from so many droid starfighters. Groodo's entire vessel explodes, and you may proceed.

If your adventure# is less than 13, subtract 7 AP from your AP total. Despite the combined firepower from twenty-five starfighters' blaster cannons, the assault has little effect against the powerful deflector shields that protect Groodo's cruiser. You must resort to more destructive tactics. To make all the droid starfighters fire their energy torpedoes at the Hutt's cruiser, roll the 20-dice again for your new roll#. Your new roll# + your navigation# + your skill# + 1 is your new adventure#.

If your new adventure# is equal to or more than 13, add the difference to your AP total. Each droid starfighter fires two energy torpedoes directly at the Hutt's cruiser. The cruiser erupts in the largest explosion you have ever seen. You may proceed.

If your new adventure# is less than 13, subtract 8 AP from your AP total. Instead of firing energy torpedoes, you accidentally instruct all twenty-five droid starfighters to convert their wings from attack mode to flight mode. Their torpedo launchers are now sealed within the protective wing assembly. To reopen the wings to attack mode, roll the 20-dice again for your new roll#. Your new roll# + your skill# is your new adventure#.

If your new adventure# is equal to or more than 12, add the difference to your AP total. All twenty-five droid starfighters revert from flight to attack mode, and the torpedo launchers are in position to fire. Go back to "roll the 20-dice again for your new roll#" and repeat. When you have destroyed the Hutt's cruiser, you may proceed.

If your new adventure# is less than 12, subtract the difference from your AP total. You failed to enter the control commands in the proper sequence. Go back to "roll the 20-dice again for your new roll#" and repeat.

You notice an emergency life pod falling away from the cruiser's wreckage. Focusing your sensors on the pod, you learn that it carries two life forms. Both Groodo the Hutt and his son have survived the destruction of their cruiser. Since Darth Sidious had specified that the Bartokks' client should live in fear, you allow the pod to tumble toward Corulag.

The twenty-five Federation droid starfighters hang like deadly ornaments in space. Although the Jedi destroyed the other twenty-five droid starfighters, Darth Sidious will be pleased that half the starfighters have been recovered.

You consider escorting the starfighters back to the Trade Federation, but you are disturbed by a single detail: your lost ally. It is highly unlikely that your ally survived the devastating explosion on Ralltiir, but you don't like the notion of the body being discovered by any enemies. You decide to return to the distant fortress and search the ruins.

First, however, you must take care of the droid starfighters. Proceed to program the droid starfighters to fly to a Neimoidian base.

To program the droid starfighters to fly to a Neimoidian base: Roll the 10-dice to send the starfighters on a programmed course through hyperspace. Your roll# + your skill# + your knowledge# is your adventure#.

If your adventure# is equal to or more than 8, add the difference + 5 to your AP total. All twenty-five droid starfighters angle in the same direction, then fire their engines and zoom off into hyperspace, on their way to the Neimoidan base. You may proceed.

If your adventure# is less than 8, subtract the difference from your AP total. You almost accidentally sent the starfighters to the planet Tatooine. Go back to "Roll the 10-dice to send the starfighters" and repeat. When the starfighters blast into hyperspace, you may proceed.

After the starfighters have left the Corulag system, you plot a course for Ralltiir.

Then you punch the controls for hyperdrive, and your starship blasts into hyperspace.

As you travel to Ralltiir, your thoughts turn to Groodo the Hutt. Darth Sidious had been confident that the Bartokks' client would somehow be useful if he were to live in fear of the Trade Federation, but you wonder . . . *Are Hutts really afraid of anything?*

By returning the droid starfighters to Trade Federation control, you have completed all of your goals. Add 200 AP to your AP total.

To read the end of this adventure, turn to page 89 of your Star Wars Adventures novel *The Fury of Darth Maul.*